THE MANY ADVENTURES OF
Johnny Mutton

STORIES AND PICTURES
BY JAMES PROIMOS

HARCOURT, INC.

SAN DIEGO   NEW YORK   LONDON

www.harcourt.com

Library of Congress Cataloging-in-Publication Data
Proimos, James.
The many adventures of Johnny Mutton/stories and pictures by James Proimos.
p.   cm.
Summary: Although he is a sheep, Johnny Mutton goes to school, competes
in the spelling bee, dresses up for Halloween, and discovers his favorite
sport, always remaining true to himself.
[1. Sheep—Fiction.   2. Schools—Fiction.   3. Individuality—Fiction.]
I. Title.
PZ7.P9432Man   2001
[Fic]—dc21   00-9219
ISBN 0-15-202379-8   ISBN 0-15-202413-1 (pb)

First edition

A C E G H F D B
A C E G H F D B (pb)

Printed in Hong Kong

The illustrations in this book were first drawn with a pen,
then colorized in Adobe Photoshop.
The display type was set in Heatwave.
The text type was set in Sand.
Printed by South China Printing Company, Ltd., Hong Kong
This book was printed on totally chlorine-free Nymolla Matte Art paper.
Production supervision by Sandra Grebenar and Ginger Boyer
Designed by Kaelin Chappell and James Proimos
Jacket/cover designed by Barry Age

For Annie and Jimmy

The Stories

Baby Steps

One day Momma Mutton opened her front door and found that a baby had been left on her front step.

But it wasn't just any baby.

It was a baby...

...sheep!

But Momma's weak eyes and warm heart kept her from even noticing.

MY, MY, MY. THE ANGELS HAVE LEFT ME A BEAUTIFUL BABY BOY!

GOO·BY DOO·BY DOO.

I WILL NAME YOU JOHNNY MUTTON AND RAISE YOU AS IF YOU WERE MY OWN.

MA. MA.

Over time, Momma Mutton taught Johnny to walk...

RIGHT FOOT, LEFT FOOT, RIGHT FOOT, LEFT FOOT...

and to talk...

SAY CHEESE.

LIMBURGER.

and to brush his teeth...

DO LIKE SO.

and to wash behind his ears.

HEY, WHEN'S THE LAST TIME YOU WASHED BEHIND YOUR EARS? I FOUND THIS POTATO GROWING BACK THERE.

GET OUT!

Although Johnny often got those last two confused.

Momma did such a good job bringing up Johnny that although folks noticed he was different, no one noticed he was a sheep.

THERE'S SOMETHING ODD ABOUT THAT BOY.

MR. STOCKMAN

HE'S VERY HAPPY. MAYBE THAT'S WHAT MAKES HIM STAND OUT.

LORETTA SMATZ

HE DOESN'T EVEN TRY TO FIT IN. I DON'T LIKE THAT.

HE'S SO HIM.

MRS. TORPOLLI

I NOTICED HE WAS DIFFERENT RIGHT AWAY. HE'S A GOOD PETTER.

THE SMITHS' DOG

Every single night before Johnny went to bed, Momma would give him the most wonderful bear hug and say...

I LOVE YOU, JOHNNY MUTTON! THERE IS NO ONE QUITE LIKE YOU.

And she certainly was right.

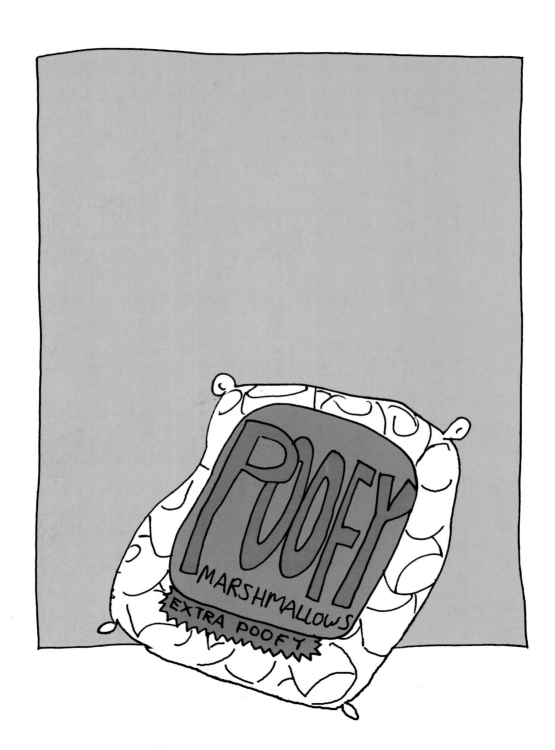

9

The students each brought their teacher, Mr. Slopdish, an apple.

All the kids laughed.

But Mr. Slopdish was pleased.

I HAVE THESE FAKE TEETH, AND THEY'RE NOT GOOD FOR EATING APPLES.

I SEE.

OF COURSE, THEY'RE JUST RIGHT FOR EATING MARSHMALLOWS.

OH MY.

But Johnny didn't hear that because he was in the closet, hiding from those creepy fake teeth.

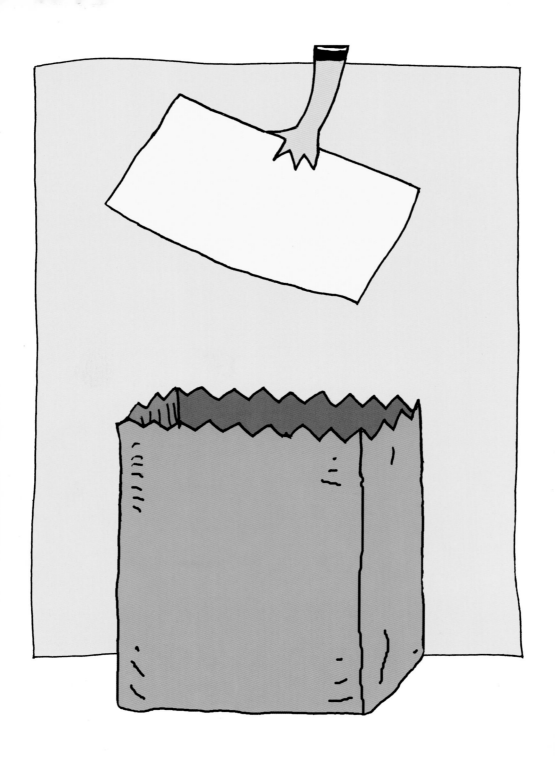

Spell Binding

There was a big spelling bee at Johnny Mutton's school. The parents of all the children came to watch.

Kids were dropping like flies.

18

Next it was Johnny's turn. But just as his teacher was reaching in the bag to pull out his word, the bell rang. The spelling bee would have to be continued the next day.

RING!
RI

YOU WERE GREAT.

WE HAVE TO STUDY ALL NIGHT. I HAVE TO WIN.

But Monday night was Momma's tuba practice night, which she never missed. "Some things are more important than winning," said Momma.

The next day the spelling bee resumed.

READY?

READY.

Everyone anxiously waited to see what word would be picked for Johnny to spell.

LOVE

Mandy Dinkus nearly croaked.

NO FAIR. TOO EASY!

The Pirates Meet the Runny Nose

It was the week before Halloween, and Johnny Mutton was even happier than usual.

MOMMA, THESE SOCKS ARE THE GREENEST AND THE LONGEST.

THE KIDS ARE GONNA LOVE MY COSTUME!

OF COURSE THEY WILL LOVE YOUR OUTFIT.

YEAH, I SAID THAT.

BUT WHAT ARE YOU DRESSING UP AS?

IT'S A SECRET!

SHHH.

WELL, JUST DON'T SCARE ME.

OH, I WON'T.

HEE HEE

When Johnny got to school, he proudly entered his classroom.

FEAST YOUR EYES ON THE GIANT RUNNY SCHNOZ!

But one witch said...

HOW STRANGE.

And a pirate said...

WHERE'S YOUR RUBBER SWORD, BUDDY?

Then an almost identical pirate said...

WHAT KIND OF GET UP IS THAT?

This all had Johnny confused and feeling icky. He had to use all his mutton powers just to keep from crying.

DON'T BLUBBER. DON'T BLUBBER.

But just then, Gloria Crust walked in. (Gloria was always late.)

FEAST YOUR EYES ON THE GIANT BOX OF TISSUES!

She loved Johnny's costume.

I LIKE YOUR STYLE, MUTTON.

LIKEWISE, CRUST.

And ever since, they've been best friends.

To Dribble or Not to Dribble

Momma Mutton was a great basketball player.

She wanted Johnny Mutton to be a
great basketball player, too.
So every day she would throw
him a hundred passes.

And every day a hundred passes would bounce off his fluffy body.

Actually, he did catch one of her passes. But it was an accident.

And that's exactly what he did.

Johnny Mutton went on to become a national hero by winning twenty gold medals in the Olympics for water ballet.

Mr. Slopdish wound up famous for telling stories about Johnny Mutton on TV talk shows. Eventually he became the Poofy Marshmallow spokesperson— his face on every bag.

They Now?

The Halloween after Johnny won those twenty gold medals, all the kids in this book dressed up as Johnny Mutton.

Except for Gloria Crust and Johnny Mutton, that is. Gloria dressed up as a mop. Johnny, as a nasty spill.

A FUZZY BUG

A WINDSHIELD WIPER

Momma continued to find many interesting items on her front step. But never again would she come across anything quite as wonderful as Johnny Mutton.

A DIAMOND RING

A FOUR-LEAF CLOVER

A MONEY-BACK GUARANTEE

A DOLL'S SHOE